nat tate

Nat Tate, London, 1959

AN AMERICAN ARTIST
1928–1960

WILLIAM BOYD

BLOOMSBURY

LONDON · BERLIN · NEW YORK · SYDNEY

This edition published in 2011

Copyright © William Boyd 1998

The moral right of the author has been asserted

First published in 1998 by 21 Publishing Ltd
31 Storeys Way, Cambridge CB3 0DP

Bloomsbury Publishing Plc, 36 Soho Square, London W1D 3QY
Bloomsbury USA, 175 5th Avenue, New York, NY 10010

www.bloomsbury.com
www.bloomsburyusa.com

Bloomsbury Publishing, London, Berlin, New York and Sydney
A CIP catalogue record for this book is available from the British Library
Library of Congress Cataloging-in-Publication data has been applied for

ISBN 978 1 4088 1446 8 (UK edition)
ISBN 978 1 60819 580 0 (US edition)

10 9 8 7 6 5 4 3 2 1

Typeset in Monotype Bodoni by Hewer Text UK Ltd, Edinburgh
Printed and bound in China by C&C Offset Printing Co., Ltd.

Acknowledgements

I would like to thank Sally Felzer for making available notes, photographs and documentation that her late sister had compiled about Nat Tate. I am grateful to the Alice Singer Gallery in New York, and Sander-Lynde Institute, Philadelphia, for permission to reproduce, respectively, *Bridge no. 122* and *Portrait of K*. The help and encouragement provided by Gudrun Ingridsdottir (administrator of the Estate of Logan Mountstuart) has been invaluable.

For Susan

I still don't know what made me climb the stairs to Alice Singer's 57th Street gallery. It was June 1997, New York City. The show was titled, 'Crowding the Air – American Drawing 1900–1990', and it seemed impossibly ambitious for her smallish space. Furthermore, the notices of it which I had read in the *Times* and the *New Yorker* disdainfully prefigured one's natural prejudices. It was late afternoon, I was hot and I was tired and I wandered past dozens of unremarkable drawings and sketches – a Feininger, a Warhol shoe, a Twombly doodle caught my eye – before I was held and shocked by something I had never expected to see. It was a drawing, 12" × 8", in ink, mixed media and collage: *Bridge no. 122*. I did not need to read the printed label beside it to know it was by Nat Tate.

It was undated, but I knew it must have been executed in the early 1950s, part of his once legendary, now almost entirely forgotten series of drawings inspired by Hart Crane's great poem, *The Bridge*. All the drawings in this series – and it

Nat Tate, *Bridge no. 122*

was reputed to run eventually to over 200 – were of similar format: at the top was the boldly stylised representation of a bridge, sometimes a tangle of girders, sometimes a simple arc, and on the bottom two thirds or half of the page was accumulated a sort of clutter or litter – slashing ink strokes, or furious cross-hatching, occasional half-representational figures, sometimes obscenely graffito-like, sometimes finely and carefully drawn, or lettering, or pasted letters, illustrations torn from magazines, skilfully juxtaposed collages in a style reminiscent of Kurt Schwitters. 'I like bridges,' Nat Tate once told an acquaintance, 'so strong, so simple – but imagine what flows in the river underneath.'

The acquaintance to whom these words had been confided was the British writer and critic Logan Mountstuart (1906–1991 – whose journals I am currently editing[1]). Mountstuart is a curious and forgotten figure in the annals of twentieth-century literary life. 'A man of letters' is probably the only description which does justice to his strange career – by turns acclaimed or wholly indigent. Biographer, belle-lettriste, editor, failed novelist, he was perhaps most successful at happening to be in the right place at the right time during most of the century, and his journal – a huge, copious document – will probably prove his lasting memorial. Mountstuart lived in New York from 1947-71 and his extensive journals provide a remarkably candid and intimate portrait of the Manhattan artistic and literary circles in which he moved. Indeed even my own patchy and conflicting account of Nat Tate's life and times – full of ambiguities and contention – could not have been compiled without the Mountstuart journals and the letters between Mountstuart and Janet Felzer[2], the dealer who first showed Tate's work in her lower Manhattan 'co-op' gallery in 1952.

Mountstuart met Nat Tate in that year and saw him from time to time thereafter. Although he could not be described as a close friend, Mountstuart was also a patron – he owned several Tate drawings, three from the *Bridge* sequence, and at least two of the larger, later paintings – and was a regular visitor to Tate's studio on 22nd Street and Lexington Avenue, a rare honour. Tate, by nature a diffident and awkward personality, seemed curiously at ease with Mountstuart (at least by Mountstuart's account). Mountstuart himself thought this was because he was British – and therefore 'foreign' – and also because he knew Europe and European artists. Nat Tate visited Europe only once in his short life, a trip he had both dreaded and longed for.

Nathwell – 'Nat' – Tate was born on the 7th March 1928, probably in Union Beach, New Jersey. His mother, Mary (née Tager), told him his father had been a fisherman from Nantucket who had drowned at sea before Nat had been born. The regular contradictions and elaborations of Mary Tate's story (Nathwell senior was variously a submariner, a naval architect, a merchant seaman killed 'in a war', a deep sea diver) later convinced his son that he was in fact illegitimate. However, there was in all the versions a link with the sea and, with ominous symbolism, the death was always the same – drowning. The only relative Mary Tate appeared to have was an aunt in Union Beach, whom Nat recalled visiting a few times. In his darker moments he fantasised that his mother had been a dockside whore and that he was the product of a swift and carnal midnight coupling with a sailor. Hence, he argued, the consistency of the identities she bestowed on his father. Whether this man was still alive, or who he actually was, Nat would clearly never know. He decided that his mother had had, in her imagination, his father 'drowned' as a punishment and as a mark of her own shame. It is plausible, though perhaps a little fanciful, to find some psychological sources here for the *Bridge* drawings: to see the bridges – simple, clear, strong – as a way of traversing safely the dark and turbulent water below, to walk, unsmirched and untouched, over the rebarbative flotsam and jetsam on the river bed beneath.

Whatever the identity of the mysterious Nathwell Tate senior, Mary Tager took his name, referred to herself as

13

Nat Tate, aged nine, in the gardens of Windrose, 1937

Mrs Nathwell Tate, and pointedly described herself to anyone who asked as a widow. She remains a shadowy figure: 'I remember my mother was a great polisher of glasses,' Tate once recalled to Mountstuart, 'perhaps she once worked in a bar . . .'. In any event she was a good housekeeper and she moved with her little boy to Peconic, Long Island, where she found work with Peter and Irina Barkasian as a kitchen maid, later being promoted to cook. Nat Tate was three years old, it was 1931, Peconic was his first real home; he had no memories of any life before Peconic and he had no idea where Mary Tate had moved from.

Peter Barkasian was a wealthy man: his father Dusan Barkasian had built up a logging and timber business into the conglomerate known as Albany Paper Mills. On his father's death in 1927, Peter immediately, and presciently, sold Albany Paper to Du Pont Chemicals and retired (aged 36) to live comfortably on the proceeds. The 1929 crash left him unscathed and his finances intact.

He bought a small but elegant summer house, Windrose, on the north fork of Long Island, where he and Irina lived in some style. Windrose was a curiosity: built in the 1890s, it was loosely modelled on the Petit Trianon and was designed by an architect called Fairfield Douglas who had worked for a while in the firm of Richard Morris Hunt. Barkasian had two long wings added in the same white stucco, neo-classical manner, had the garden re-landscaped and a small hill bull-dozed flat to afford a better southern view of Peconic Bay.

Windrose, Fairfield Douglas

More than two thousand trees and ornamental shrubs were planted. His 'retirement' was to be in the grandest style. The couple were childless: Irina concerned herself with local charities; Peter, cash rich in the Depression, travelled to New York once a week, where he diligently managed his portfolio of stocks and shares and established a small reputation as a connoisseur and collector – Tiffany lamps were his particular passion, but he also bought and sold pictures in a modest way and he had a fine collection of John Marin watercolours.

The eastern reaches of Long Island in the 1930s presented a picture of bleakness and deprivation: flat potato fields and isolated village communities of clam and scallop fishers, many of which still did not have electricity. Here and there were pockets of more cosmopolitan activity. East Hampton and Amagansett, on the south shore, had been attracting

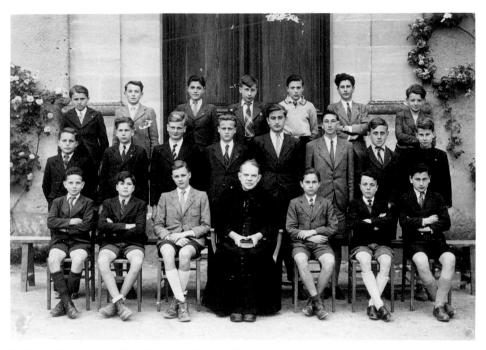

Nat Tate, aged sixteen, at Briarcliff, middle row, fourth from the right

artists for decades, but Peconic, on the north of the bay, was on the wrong side of the tracks, artistically speaking, or 'below the bridge', as the local expression ran. Windrose seemed to be a rich man's folly, but Peter Barkasian did not care: it was his own world, bought and paid for.

Mary Tate was killed by a speeding delivery van as she stepped out of a drugstore in Riverhead, Long Island, one February morning in 1936. Nat was eight years old. He recalled to Mountstuart that he learnt of his mother's death when a boy leaned out of a window overlooking the schoolyard where he was playing and bawled, 'Hey, Tate, your mom's been run over by a truck.' He thought it was a cruel joke, shrugged and carried on with his softball game. It was only when he saw the headmaster grimly crossing the playground towards him that he realised he was an orphan.

It was natural – inevitable? – that the Barkasians should adopt Mary Tate's orphan boy; it was also Nat Tate's first substantial stroke of good fortune, if the enormous personal tragedy of the loss of one's mother can be looked at in such a way. Little is known of the next few years, unfamiliarly cosseted and privileged as they must have been. 'I hated my adolescence,' he once cryptically told Mountstuart, 'all spunk and shame', and he never talked much about his teenage years or about the boarding school he was sent to – Briarcliff in Connecticut, now defunct. There is a poignant and touching photograph of him at home in Peconic on a holiday (it can't have been long after his mother's death). The boy, standing on a lawn, awkward, arms akimbo, looking away from the camera, the new soccer ball on the grass between his feet, perhaps kicked over towards him by a genial Peter Barkasian, learning to be a 'Dad'. A few years later (in 1944) a more formal pose reveals the sixteen-year-old standing behind the left shoulder of the Dean of Briarcliff (Reverend Davis Trigg). Nat's unsmiling face, plump with puppy fat, this time seems to stare out at the camera resentfully, his thick butter-blond hair scraped back from his forehead in a damp, disciplined lick.

Academically, Nat did not excel. The only subject that engaged him was art, or 'Paint and Drawing' as it was known at Briarcliff. Nat did graduate but his grades were disappointing – only in 'Paint and Drawing' was he an 'A' student. And at this stage of his life his second stroke of luck occurred. Keen to capitalise on any vestige of a gift that his son might display, Peter Barkasian managed to have Nat enrolled in an art school, the celebrated Hofmann Summer School – which moved from its downtown Manhattan base each summer to Provincetown, Massachusetts. Nat never attended classes at West 9th Street in Manhattan, but for the four summers of 1947–51 he studied under the eccentric but vigorously modern tutelage of Hans Hofmann in the small fishing village on Cape Cod Bay.

Hans Hofmann was a German émigré who had come to America in 1930. A big, blustering man with an adamantine ego and sense of mission, he was steeped in European

Hans Hofmann

Modernism and armed with redoubtable and abstruse theories about the integrity of the two-dimensional plane of the canvas. Its 'flatness' was its defining feature, and the artist's sole task was to respect this as he arranged his coloured pigments upon it. Paint was 'inert', representation was wrongheaded, abstraction was God. In the '40s and the '50s, Hofmann's dogmatic asseverations, delivered at his art school in downtown Manhattan and in the summer in Provincetown, profoundly influenced a whole generation of American artists.

At Provincetown, Nat Tate was still socially ill-at-ease during those Cape Cod summers, shy and unsure of himself. He did not mix much with the other students, guilty, so he told Mountstuart, about being so well off, and he is barely remembered by any of the school's more celebrated alumni. He dressed soberly, almost old-fashionedly, in jackets and ties (a habit he was never fully to abandon), worked hard and, out of classroom hours, kept himself largely to himself.

Hans Hofmann's Summer School in Provincetown, 1956. Photograph by Arnold Newman

Nat Tate's studio at Windrose

For the rest of the year he lived with the Barkasians. Peter
was excited by the genuine talent that Nat was showing, and
for the first time, one senses, he truly began to take an
interest in his adopted son, renovating and transforming a
small summer-house in the garden at Windrose, which Nat
used as a studio and den. Logan Mountstuart observed that
'although Nat has two parents he only ever talks about
Peter – Peter this, Peter that – Irina was there, somewhere,
but always in the distant background; it was as if, now Nat
had left school, her role was over and Peter stepped in.' Janet
Felzer, in a letter to Mountstuart in 1961, put it more bluntly:

'the fact was that during the Provincetown years Peter B. slowly but surely fell in love with his son.'

Whether Felzer's assessment is true or false, the relationship between the two grew closer. Peter Barkasian paid Nat a generous monthly allowance in return for which he was given all the art that Nat wished to see preserved. In 1950 Barkasian began to catalogue every sketch and painting he received. Each work was labelled, dated and, if not hung, was stored carefully away in a strong room in the main house. Felzer again: 'Peter thought he had a genius working at the bottom of the garden – so he started to log and collect his output for posterity.'

No one knows when Nat Tate began his *Bridge* sequence of
drawings, or why he was so taken with the Hart Crane poem[3].
The best guess puts it some time in 1950. Certainly by the time
Janet Felzer first saw some of the drawings in 1952 their
numberings were already up in the eighties and nineties.

Felzer was driving back from Long Island to New York – she
had been weekending in Southampton – with the poet and
critic Frank O'Hara. They stopped for a drink in Islip and,
killing some time, wandered into a local gallery there, which
happened to be run by a friend of Peter Barkasian (from
whom Barkasian had bought two Winslow Homer watercolours, it seemed). Half a dozen of Nat Tate's *Bridge*
drawings were hung in a back room.

Cambridge, Mass., 1947. Left to right: Janet Felzer, Logan
Mountstuart, Unknown, Franz Kline, and 'Pablo' the Norwich
terrier.

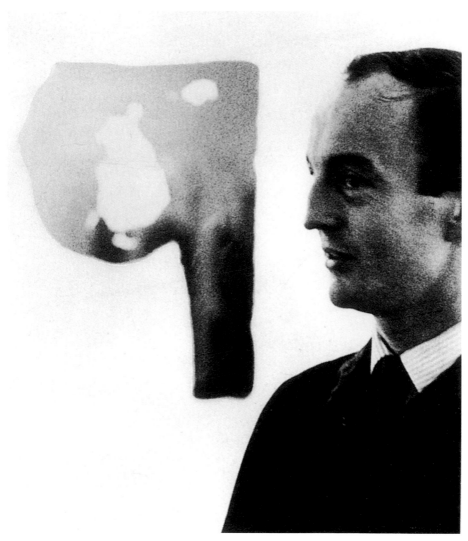

Frank O'Hara, c. 1955

Hart Crane

Janet Felzer (1922–1977) was an energetic and influential
figure in the New York gallery world of the 1950s. A
moderately talented painter herself (she had studied in
Rome), she founded one of the early co-op galleries in the
late '40s called Aperto. The co-op galleries were a short-lived
phenomenon, vaguely inspired, as the name indicates, by the
concept of a guild or brotherhood, established by groups of
young and little known artists who wanted a space to show
their work. They each made a contribution to the running
costs and were thereby entitled to hang their paintings on
the gallery's walls – usually a downtown loft or warehouse
space. The most famous of the co-op galleries was in Jane
Street in Greenwich Village where Larry Rivers first showed.

Aperto moved two or three times in its short life before it
settled in an old peanut factory in Hudson Street. Its
co-operative status soon became purely nominal as Janet
Felzer herself took over the running costs, and although
certain artists could claim to belong to the Aperto group (and

made erratic financial contributions) it was essentially run and owned by Felzer herself. Janet Felzer possessed an eclectic and modern taste which governed her choice of artists, but she most favoured those with some overt intellectual heft (Jackson Pollock left her 'cold as a glacier', she said). She recognised the Hart Crane debt in Tate's powerful, intense drawings and was immediately captivated. 'That Crane fellow should charge you a commission,' Franz Kline once jokingly observed to Nat when he later became a *succès fou*. 'Hart is dead,' Nat replied, flatly, 'so it doesn't matter.' Kline denied this heatedly and fiercely until he was advised they were talking about Hart – not Art. (Mountstuart witnessed this droll exchange in, appropriately, the Cedar Tavern.)

The fact that Felzer was with Frank O'Hara, himself a poet (and an admirer of Crane's work), seems to have consolidated her instinctive enthusiasm for the drawings. O'Hara was a fascinating and central figure of the New York art scene of the 1950s and '60s. A homosexual with a slight, elfin figure and a conspicuous hooked nose, he – like the poet John Ashbery – was a key link in the chain that bound the world of literature to that of contemporary painting. O'Hara was a published poet and also worked at the Museum of Modern Art as a curator. A garrulous but beguiling nature made him a popular figure – his premature death in an auto accident in 1966 robbed the art world of one of its most singular presences.

Encouraged by O'Hara's enthusiasm, Felzer retrieved Nat Tate's address and phone number from the gallery owner and

Janet Felzer, 1954

the two returned to New York brimful with excitement and gleeful self-satisfaction at their discovery.

Logan Mountstuart's journal:

> July 10 [1952] . . . Frank was there, impish and irritating, drunk as a skunk and deeply tanned. For half an hour he had me pinned in a corner yodelling on about some barbarian genius called Pate [sic] he had unearthed in Long Island. 'At last an artist with a brain, thank gaaaahhhhd.' Back to Janet's place . . .

Mountstuart was having an affair with Janet Felzer at the time, a lengthy and tormented relationship that over the years knew many periods of chill and hostility before somehow reviving fervidly. In his journals Mountstuart is convinced that Nat Tate and Janet slept together in 1952 'on at least three separate' occasions, though no one else can confirm that this ever took place. Felzer was a dark vivacious woman, always fashionably dressed, and with pronounced cheekbones that gave her an exotic, Slavonic look. She went everywhere with an ill-disciplined, yapping Norwich terrier she called Pablo ('Pablo drove us apart again and again,' Mountstuart confessed, 'he was, finally, the victor.')

The 1952 Aperto Gallery show marks the start of Nat Tate's brief encounter with fame. Hanging with him were pictures by Barnett Newman, Lee Krasner, Todd Heuber and Adolf Gottlieb. Clement Greenberg wrote in the short-lived

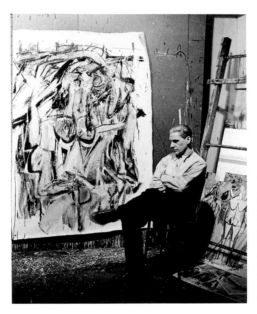

handbill *AtR* (destined to fail, according to Mountstuart, with such a crass title, as well as being distributed free): '. . . and there were some promising, oddly disturbing drawings by Nat Tate, though he would be well advised to pay fewer visits to Mr de Kooning's studio.' As Janet Felzer angrily pointed out, Nat Tate had been working in almost complete isolation, apart from his exposure to other painters at the Hofmann Summer School. None of the rampant cross-fertilisation currently taking place in the New York art scene of the early '50s could be applied to him. Indeed, while Tate was notionally a member of the 'New York School' and at the end of his life what might be termed an Abstract

Peter
Barkasian

Expressionist, his pictures are always sidelined, or differentiated, by their idiosyncracies. He was both like and very unlike his contemporaries. However, what caused most astonishment was that all of Tate's drawings were sold before the show officially opened. Janet Felzer later told Mountstuart that Peter Barkasian had made it a condition of Nat's participation that he should have first refusal on all his work – and naturally he bought them entire.

Logan Mountstuart's journal:

November 5th. Gunpowder Treason and Plot at J's gallery. Annoyingly, the show seems to be a wild success. Frank

Left to right: John Ashbery, Frank O'Hara, Patsy Southgate, Bill Berkson, Kenneth Koch with lamp sculpture by Larry Rivers, 1964

raving boringly on about his 'discovery' – everything sold
in a flash. I met this prodigy later. A quiet tall handsome
boy who reminded me of Ulrich [a friend of Mountstuart
from the period of his incarceration in Switzerland,
1944–45]. He stood quietly in a corner, drinking Scotch,
wearing a grey suit. Heavy dark blond hair. Janet was
on fire, said she had been smoking heroin (can one do
this?) and offered me some. I said I was too old for those
games. Bumped into Tate again as I was leaving and
complimented him on his work. I asked if he had anything
else for sale and he said – most oddly – that I would have
to ask his father. Later Pablo shat copiously in the middle
of the room, so Larry Rivers told me.

Frank O'Hara with Franz Kline at the Cedar Tavern, March 1959

Janet Felzer abandoned the Aperto Gallery in Hudson Street and moved uptown to Madison Avenue (and 78th Street) where she opened the Janet Felzer Gallery in 1954 with another landmark show including works by Philip Guston, William Baziotes and Martha Heuber (Todd's sister). Nat Tate moved north with Janet Felzer, and in the 1954 exhibition he had one large solitary canvas called *White Building*. This announced the start of another sequence, this time in oil, a series of façades of a house with crudely painted doors and windows in black almost invisible under a screen of thinned white oil paint. 'Like ghost houses,' Mountstuart remarked. The deliberate monochrome was again individual, owing nothing to Kline, Motherwell or de Kooning – with the first of whom Nat had now become friendly. They were in fact, as Mountstuart recognised, images of Windrose, painted from photographs, of a large size (5′×8′) and, according to Janet

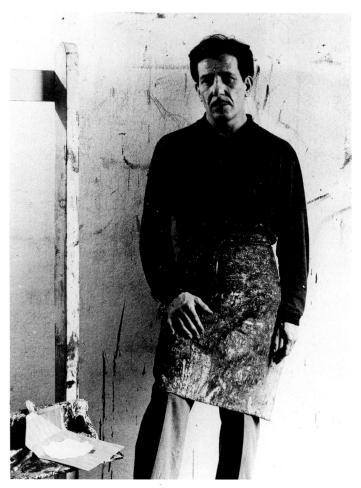

Franz Kline, 1956

Felzer, Nat completed 'at least eight or ten' over the next few years. Barkasian bought them all, hanging them in sequence in the capacious entrance hall at the house, where they were, reputedly, most impressive. None has survived.

Mountstuart was a particular admirer of the *White Building* sequence, intrigued by the way the much erased and repainted and then overpainted simplifications of window embrasure, arch, column, frieze and portico somehow defied obliteration by the layers of white, turps-thinned oil paint that was repeatedly laid over them. What looked like a scumbled and overworked gesso field with blurry grey/black markings revealed itself, after some moments of staring, 'to be a real record of a real house in a real place'. Mountstuart thought also that these spectral canvases 'were a profound statement of time and time passing, of the brave refusal of man's artefacts to be completely overwhelmed by oblivion'.

The mid '50s marks the period of Mountstuart's closest contacts with Nat Tate. He weekended at Windrose several times and came to know the Barkasians. The photo of an uncomfortable looking Peter Barkasian on the beach at Fire Island was taken by Logan Mountstuart in 1957. A measure of this new relaxation was the sale to Mountstuart of three drawings from the *Bridge* sequence. Barkasian realised that he could not, with Nat's mounting renown, maintain a monopoly on the artist's work. Consequently, Janet Felzer was allowed to sell a few drawings and some gouache studies for the *White Building* oils. As Nat Tate's profile was steadily raised there were many more offers made than there were works available. Nat was not a fast or prolific artist, indeed it was sufficient for him merely to show from time to time; unlike most of his contemporaries he had no economic incentive: Barkasian's generous allowance was maintained and he paid Janet Felzer the market rates for Nat's work and, as Felzer explained to Mountstuart, she could hardly complain. In terms of the commission she made, Nat Tate was virtually her most successful artist. Even so, she continued to encourage and push him, persisting with the idea of a solo show, but Nat was reluctant, happy merely to hang with other artists in her gallery.

This was, perhaps, the period of his life when he was at his most content, accepted and admired by his peers, finally free of Windrose, living on his own in Manhattan, with a lively group of artists and friends, most of whom were savouring the fruits of their success and international acclaim. Nat

Peter Barkasian on the beach at Fire Island, 1957. © The Estate of Logan Mountstuart, 1958

Tate cut a slightly different figure from his peers – a tall, fit-looking young man, he was well groomed, disdaining the jeans and dungarees favoured by other artists of the New York School. In the summer he was always deeply tanned, Mountstuart remembered, also commenting that he seemed to choose his clothes with care – such as midnight-blue suits with cream linen shirts – and that he had a predilection for light, self-coloured ties, ivory, silver-grey, pale banana yellow. He was handsome – and he knew it – but there was nothing predatory or narcissistic about him. 'Sometimes he seemed almost embarrassed by the stares he attracted from both males and females,' Janet Felzer noted, 'as if to say "Why are they looking at me? What have I done now?"'

By the mid-1950s, the era of Abstract Expressionism and Action Painting was well under way. Jackson Pollock and Willem de Kooning led the pack, closely followed by other artists such as David Smith, Franz Kline and Robert Motherwell. The New York School was into its well-heeled, drink-fuelled, fame-driven stride. Like many artistic movements that claim the attention of the media, a deal of self-conscious myth-making occurred and stereotypes duly emerged (the artist as visionary drunk, the artist as surly macho brute, the artist as brawling suffering genius), as well as many a brief minor talent, seeking their moment of glory. Much of the initial socialising – the drinking, the talking, the sex – centred around the Cedar Tavern on University Place and 8th Street in Greenwich Village.

Regulars at the Cedar Tavern, 24 University Place, October 1959

Frank O'Hara at the Museum of Modern Art with (left) Roy
Lichtenstein and (right) Henry Geldzahler

As Elaine de Kooning said, 'around 1950 everyone just got
drunk and the whole art world went on a long, long bender.'
The Cedar Tavern, a drab, shabby place (which is still there,
still remarkably authentic), is in a way the symbolic artefact
of the period – playing the kind of role the Café Flore does
in the annals of left-bank Parisian Existentialism – eternally
conjuring up an image of famous artists drinking at the bar,
talking and quarrelling about art, turkeycocking, eyeing up
the art groupies that were drawn to the place, curiously
circling them. It was a charged, exciting time, and for Nat
Tate a first real taste of escape, of true independence. Like
everybody else, like every other artist he met, Nat began
drinking heavily, joining the long, long bender that was
going on around him. Gore Vidal met him at this time and

remembered him as an 'essentially dignified drunk with nothing to say. Unlike most American painters, he was unverbal. "He was a great lover," Peggy Guggenheim told me years later. "Almost in a class with Sam Beckett who had bad skin. I loved Sam for six months. A record for me. Nat for – oh, six weeks at the outside." [4]

For Nat Tate, Frank O'Hara remained a mentor-figure and friend. It is not clear if they were ever lovers (O'Hara was living with Joe LeSueur from 1955) but the relationship took on more professional dimensions when O'Hara, as curator, selected two of the *White Building* paintings for the 4th São Paulo Bienal in 1957. There is an uncollected poem O'Hara wrote around that time called *What if we hadn't had such great names?* that captures some of the flavour of those heady days in the '50s, when the art world looked to New York for its inspiration, and the city's artists, it seemed, could do no wrong.

> What if we hadn't had such great names?
> What if we had been called
> Gilbert Kline, Jonathan Pollock, Cyril
> O'Hara, Jennifer Krasner, Timothy Rivers,
> Philip Tate?. . .
> We were lucky people, lucky to be living
> then and in NYC. *Quelle chance!* Lucky
> (watch out posterity, here we come!)
> that we had such great names.

Mountstuart, however, decided that Nat Tate and O'Hara were in fact lovers – however temporary – and confided as much to his journal on, it has to be said, the slimmest of evidence. In 1958, out of four visits he made to Nat's 22nd Street studio, O'Hara happened to be there three times. Circumstantial evidence, perhaps, but Mountstuart was always inclined to rush to judgement, and he never really liked O'Hara, distrusting his loquacity and envying his popularity.

Early in 1959, however, there seems to have been some cooling off between Tate and O'Hara (largely on O'Hara's side, prompted by Barkasian's refusal to lend any Tates for O'Hara's 'Documenta II' show in Kassel, West Germany), and Mountstuart began to see more of Nat. The artist was still drinking heavily, Mountstuart recorded (no mean imbiber himself, so it must have been unignorably copious), and there is a possibility that Tate merely saw the British writer as a stalwart and congenial drinking companion. None the less, it was about this time that Mountstuart bought (for $2,000 and $2,750) two canvases from what was dubbed the 'Third Panel Triptych' period of Nat Tate's work.

Logan Mountstuart's journal:

April 23. To Nat's around 6 p.m. to collect *Still Life no. 5*. He was already quite drunk and kept repeating that Janet was to know nothing about this sale. I reassured him. We went into the studio where I watched him at work

Franz Kline with Didier van Taller, 1955

for an hour. He was swigging direct from a Jack Daniel's bottle. He was working on a triptych and the final panel was primed and ready on the big easel. We listened to music (Scriabin, I think) and talked aimlessly about the forthcoming trip to France and Italy – where he should go, who he should see. Nat seemed to be waiting to reach a certain plateau of drunkenness, seemed to be waiting for the booze to trigger the precise moment. Suddenly he threw the dust sheets off the other two completed panels. There was, first, a nude, an orthodox odalisque, more yellow than flesh toned, and then, in the second panel, another version of it, more stylised and crudely flashy – very sub-de Kooning. Nat stood there staring at the two panels, drinking, and then literally attacked the big canvas with a wide brush and tubes of cadmium yellow, laying on great swathes of colour. He seemed quite deranged to me. I left after an hour with my still life and he was still at it, rubbing off most of what he had done with a rag then going hard at it again, this time with black and green.

The *Third Panel Triptychs* appeared wholly abstract, painted in a kind of drunken frenzy, even though they were purported copies of the first two panels which were more orthodoxly representational, and which explains their run-of-the-mill figurative titles – *Sag Harbour Sunset, Still life with Baseball Mitt, Yellow Nude, Portrait of K* (possibly Kenneth Koch). When the third panel was completed to his satisfaction, Nat destroyed the other two – thus erasing the sources and breaking the causal chain forever. Peter Barkasian did not

44

Nat Tate, *Portrait of K*, 1958, 91.44 × 121.92 cm. The Sander-Lynde Institute, Philadelphia

like this direction his protégé's painting was taking (perhaps he was aware of the *dérèglement de sens* which was involved in their composition) and for the first time Janet Felzer was able to sell Nat's work more widely, five or six of the *Third Panel Triptychs* going to private clients and at least one to a public gallery of twentieth-century art (the Sander-Lynde Institute, Philadelphia).

A measure of this wider distribution and his growing renown was the irruption into Nat Tate's life of the notorious dealer Didier van Taller. Van Taller was a predatory and ambiguous figure who – so he claimed – operated from a gallery in Brussels and who haunted and disrupted the New York art world intermittently throughout the late '50s and early '60s. He had made a determined effort to woo Franz Kline from his dealer Sidney Janis. Having failed in this, he now turned his attention to other members of the New York School, Nat Tate being a prime target along with Robert Motherwell and the sculptress Louise Nevelson.

Nat categorically refused to see van Taller (his loyalty to the Felzer Gallery was absolute), but, curiously, Peter Barkasian seemed to like the man and they were often seen together socially. According to Mountstuart, Nat grew very disturbed by this association, convinced that Barkasian was contemplating a large sale of his Tate holdings to van Taller (Mountstuart speculated that Barkasian was in financial difficulties – this seems unlikely, however).

Left to right: Peter Barkasian, Irina Barkasian, Didier van Taller, Unknown. New York, 1958

Logan Mountstuart, 1959

Whether it was Nat Tate's increasing alcoholic dependency, or signs of some incipient crack-up, the van Taller intrusion deeply – and irrationally – upset him, according to both Felzer and Mountstuart, and seems to have marked the beginning of his decline. In any event, no decision was taken, and no sale was made. Didier van Taller moved out of Nat's life, and in the Fall of 1959 Peter Barkasian and Nat embarked – in apparent good spirits – on their long projected trip to Europe.

Janet Felzer says they spent a fortnight in London before going to France as guests of Douglas Cooper (the celebrated collector) at the Château de Castille near Avignon, where, one memorable Sunday, they lunched with Picasso. John Richardson, who met Nat at this time, remembered: 'It was obvious that Tate had a drink problem, and there seemed to be some tension between him and Barkasian, but I found him

Pablo Picasso: 'You live a poet's life,' he told Hélène Parmelin, 'and I a convict's.'

Braque sitting at the table on the terrace of his house at
Varengeville

charming and unassuming. I don't think he spoke to Picasso
beyond saying "hello" and "goodbye". Barkasian rather hogged
Picasso, as I recall.'[5]

Cooper, who was travelling to Paris, accompanied Tate and
Barkasian north and introduced them to Georges Braque,
at Braque's house in Varengeville, Normandy.

Georges Braque, *La Terrasse*, 1948–61, oil on canvas, 97 × 130. Private Collection

Georges Braque was seventy-eight years old at the time of Tate's visit, and, along with Picasso and Matisse, one of the three great pillars of twentieth-century art. Braque, a serene, modest and genial character, was at the height of his mature powers, his great sequence of studio interiors – a chain of masterworks created over two decades and almost unrivalled in modern painting – recently completed.

According to Janet Felzer, Nat felt vastly more at ease with Braque than with Picasso and gladly accepted when Braque offered to show him around his studio. Braque was then reworking his painting *La Terrasse*, which he had begun some eleven years earlier, a fact that Tate found astonishing, not to say incomprehensible. He was also deeply moved and captivated by some of the smaller elongated landscapes and seascapes in the studio. Apparently Tate ventured the opinion that they reminded him of van Gogh's late landscapes. After gently correcting Tate's pronunciation ('*Van Go? Non, mon ami, jamais*'), Braque commented that he 'regarded van Gogh as a great painter of night.' The observation seemed to trouble Nat unduly, as if it was prophetic or gnomic in some sinister way (he reiterated it to both Felzer and Mountstuart). There is a photograph of the *fête champêtre* that Nat and Barkasian had with Braque and his family and friends during that visit, taken by Barkasian, one assumes, as he is absent from the picture. Braque himself sits at the centre of the table, dappled with autumn sunshine, while the women of the household fuss over the food and the *placement*. Nat stands close to the master, on his left, a plate in his hand,

The *fête champêtre* at Varengeville, September 1959. Georges Braque (seated centre), Nat Tate (standing to Braque's left), Mme. Braque (standing, pointing)

almost as if he is about to serve him. But his gaze is unfocused, he looks out of frame, at something in the middle distance, or perhaps just lost in his darkening thoughts. Nothing would ever be the same again.

Indeed, shortly after the visit to Varengeville, the trip to France was abruptly curtailed, the Italian segment was cancelled and Tate and Barkasian returned immediately to New York.

Logan Mountstuart's journal:

> December 4th. Nat Tate came round, unannounced, last night – not drunk, indeed quite calm and composed. He offered me $6000 for my two paintings which I declined. He said he wanted to rework them (inspired, apparently, by a visit to Braque's studio) and so I let him take them away, with some reluctance. He offered me $1500 for my three *Bridge* drawings – I said I would swop them for another painting. He became rather tetchy at this point – banging on about true artistic integrity and its conspicuous absence in NY etc etc – so I gave him a stiff drink and unhooked my two canvases from the wall, keen to see the back of him. Janet called later with a report of the same 'reworking' notion. She had given him back whatever work she had at the gallery. She thought it sounded a 'neat' idea.

Neither Mountstuart nor Felzer was ever to see Nat Tate, nor their paintings, again.

Janet Felzer, 1975

Reconstructing the last days of Nat Tate's life is problematic, but Janet Felzer made real efforts, seeking some explanation for the events that followed[6], which she communicated to Mountstuart, who duly noted the details in his journal.

Throughout December 1959 it is clear that Nat Tate tried either to buy back or asked to be allowed to 'rework' as many as possible of his paintings as were in public hands. There is no reason to doubt that he was sincere in this regard, that it was not, in Mountstuart's uncharitable words, 'little short of theft'. Nat Tate had seen Braque at work, had witnessed his tireless and dogged perfectionism at first hand, and it is entirely conceivable he was inspired by Braque's example. In any event, he locked himself away in his Windrose studio and worked uninterrupted through the holiday season and into the early days of 1960. The only people to see him at this stage were Peter and Irina Barkasian and the Windrose staff.

Something, though, went seriously wrong, either with the work, or else the heavy drinking took its toll (Tate was never a serious drug user), or else the long anticipated nervous breakdown arrived. In early January, while Peter Barkasian and Irina were away in Florida, he removed all his work from the studio, the house and the strongroom and, with the enthusiastic help of the janitor and his twelve-year-old son, burnt everything during the freezing afternoon of January 8th.

Todd Heuber, 1957

On January 10th he came to Manhattan and undertook a
similar purge on the canvases in the 22nd Street studio,
including, it is assumed, those he had taken from the Felzer
Gallery, and Mountstuart's two. With the slate wiped clean
Nat embarked afresh, it is thought, beginning work on a new
painting he entitled *Orizaba/Return to Union Beach*.

On January 12th he called on Janet Felzer at the gallery
but (to her eternal regret) she was out to lunch. He went
downtown to the Museum of Modern Art and had coffee with
Frank O'Hara and Todd Heuber who had also, coincidentally,
dropped by. Heuber had recently returned from a trip to

Scandinavia and he recalled Tate talking vaguely about going back to France and visiting Braque again. Tate only stayed about twenty minutes, O'Hara remembered, and he seemed in a composed though somewhat thoughtful mood – certainly there was nothing in his demeanour to cause alarm.

However, sometime after lunch Nat Tate bought a ticket on the Staten Island ferry. On board the ferry, a few moments before five o'clock that afternoon, a young man was observed to remove his tweed coat, hat and scarf, and walk to the stern. The ship was midway between the Statue of Liberty and the Military Ocean Terminal at Bayonne, heading for the New Jersey shore and roughly in the direction of Union Beach, where, theoretically, it had all begun. The young man climbed the guard rail, heedless of the other passengers' cries, spread his arms and leaped.

Frank O'Hara leaving the Museum of Modern Art, January 1960

Hart Crane, portrait by David Alfaro Siqueiros, from The Hart Crane Collection, Rare Book and Manuscript Library, Columbia University, New York

Nat Tate's body was never found. When news of the suicide and the circumstantial evidence – descriptions tallying, a taxi driver recalling a fare from MoMA to the ferry terminal, etc. – were collated the awful and depressing conclusions were reluctantly drawn. On the 15th January Logan Mountstuart and Jane Felzer went to Tate's 22nd Street studio only to find Peter Barkasian already there supervising the packing up of Nat's possessions.

Logan Mountstuart's journal:

> . . . the place was immaculate, tidy and ordered. In the kitchen glasses were clean and stacked, wastepaper baskets had been emptied. In the studio we saw one large canvas placed against the wall, obviously recently started, a crosshatched mass of bruised blues, purples and blacks. Its title *Orizaba/Return to Union Beach* was scrawled on the back and neither Janet or Barkasian picked up the reference. I told them that 'Orizaba' was the name of the ship that was carrying Hart Crane home from Havana on his last fatal journey in 1932. 'Fatal?' Barkasian said. 'How did he die?' Janet shrugged. I felt I had to tell him: 'He drowned,' I said, 'he jumped overboard.' Barkasian was shocked, driven to tears: the painting, inchoate and mystifying, was suddenly the only suicide note available. If poor Nat could not have contrived to live his life as an artist he at least ensured that the symbolic weight of its end was apt and to be duly noted.

Why did Nat Tate kill himself? What made him throw himself into the icy confluence of the Hudson and the East River that January day in 1960? There are many theories, some glib, some complex. Mountstuart decided initially that he had fallen into a depression, drink-fuelled perhaps – 'simply gone barking mad' – and decided to kill himself. Janet Felzer considered that there was a deeper insecurity: she always suspected something had in fact occurred between Barkasian and van Taller, some deal had been struck – which Barkasian had denied but which, perhaps, Nat had unwittingly unearthed. This was the only way she could account for the almost wholesale destruction of his work. There was a desire there to frustrate Barkasian from beyond the grave, to punish him for an unforgivable betrayal.

Standing there in Alice Singer's gallery, thirty-seven years later, looking at *Bridge no. 122*, one of perhaps a dozen works by Nat Tate that survive (and wondering if it had once been one of Logan Mountstuart's), I thought that the mystery of Nat Tate's untimely death was explained perhaps by all of these answers, and more. Nat Tate had a talent, for sure, an uncertain gift, but perhaps he knew in the core of his being that it did not amount to much. Van Taller's arrival was the presaging of a future he did not welcome. Tate was one of those rare artists who did not need, and did not seek, the transformation of his painting into a valuable commodity to be bought and sold on the whim of a market and its marketeers. He had seen the future and it stank.

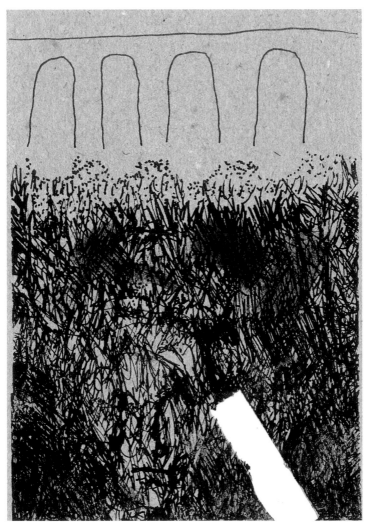

Un-numbered *Bridge* drawing, 1959. Private Collection

Larry Rivers giving the oration at Frank O'Hara's funeral, July 28, 1966. Logan Mountstuart, present amongst the two hundred mourners, wrote: 'a blazing, stifling hot day. Bizarre sight of hundreds of people in sunglasses. Larry's speech surprisingly affecting. It was as if we all felt some kind of full stop had been made to our era. Nat Tate dead at 32. O'Hara at 40. I suppose they will become our plaster saints – something to be said for dying young.'

My own feeling is that the meeting with Braque and the opportunity to see some of Braque's great final paintings removed the last supports from a person and a personality that was, by all accounts, a fragile one, however charming and easy on the eye. The example of a truly great artist at the summit of his powers will – and perhaps should – have a daunting effect on a lesser talent, particularly one still finding its way. The difference in the case of Nat Tate was that it was not so much awe or reverence or a natural sense of inadequacy that he felt – as shame. And shame was an emotion he found impossible to live with.

Logan Mountstuart later softened his brutal diagnosis, realising there were too many signs and signals about Nat's final acts for them to be incoherent and deranged. He cited the quiet guile employed in reclaiming the work, the thoroughgoing and systematic destruction of everything he could lay his hands on (99 per cent, Felzer ruefully calculated), the careful positioning of the incomplete *Orizaba* canvas with its encoded Hart Crane message, even the choice of death and its location. 'He is one whose name is writ on water,' Mountstuart commented a year or so after Nat Tate's death – very wisely, I think. 'It was all about drowning, in the end, I'm sure. Nat was drowning – literally and figuratively – and so he headed out to sea making for the Jersey shore where it all began, where he had been conceived, perhaps. There was in his suicide a great unhappy massing of symbols – of art, of blissful escape, of despair – and in his own desperate willed death by water lay a final bitter gesture towards the drowned father that he never knew.'

Notes

1

Logan Mountstuart: The Intimate Journals, edited by William Boyd, will be published in September 1999.

2

Janet Felzer's letters to Logan Mountstuart © the Estate of Logan Mountstuart 1997.

3

Hart Crane (1899–1932), American poet. Crane published only two collections of poetry in his lifetime, *White Buildings* (1926) and *The Bridge* (1930), but is still recognised as the outstanding poet of his generation. A neurotic, unstable personality, he became convinced that his creative talent had become dissipated, and he committed suicide by jumping from a ship that was bringing him home from a year's residence in Mexico.

4

Letter to the author, 1997.

5

Letter to the author, 1997.

6

This account of Nat Tate's last days was compiled by Janet Felzer in the year after his death.